FOOD AND YOU

Body Fuel
A Guide to Good Nutrition

Donna Shryer
with Stephen Dawson

Marshall Cavendish
Benchmark
New York

Marshall Cavendish Benchmark
99 White Plains Road
Tarrytown, NY 10591
www.marshallcavendish.us

Library of Congress Cataloging-in-Publication Data

Shryer, Donna.
   Body fuel : a guide to good nutrition / by Donna Shryer with Stephen Dawson.
      p. cm. — (Benchmark rockets: food and you)
   Includes index.
   Summary: "An introduction to nutrition and making healthy food choices"—Provided by publisher.
   ISBN 978-0-7614-4362-9
1. Nutrition—Juvenile literature. I. Dawson, Stephen. II. Title.

RA784.S534 2010
613.2—dc22
2008054059

Publisher: Michelle Bisson
Editorial Development and Book Design: Trillium Publishing, Inc.

Photo research by Trillium Publishing, Inc.

Cover photo: iStockphoto.com/Kelly Cline

The photographs and illustrations in this book are used by permission and through the courtesy of: *Shutterstock.com*: Morgan Lane Photography, 1, 9; Oguz Aral, 6 (diagram); Stephen Coburn, 6 (pizza); Igor Dutina, 19; Elena Elisseeva, 24; Mandy Godbehear, 27. iStockphoto.com: Stockphoto4u, 3; ABImages, 13; Chris Bence, 17. *Corbis*: LWA-Stephen Welstead/Corbis, 4. *USDA*: 8. *The Wheat Foods Council*: 11; *Superstock, Inc.*: 14. *Stockxpert*: 20.

Printed in Malaysia
1 3 5 6 4 2

Contents

1 All about Nutrition

Nutrition is an art. It is also a science. It takes creativity to keep a healthy diet interesting and appealing. It also takes knowledge to understand what foods are best for your body. Vending machines and fast-food drive-throughs are everywhere. It would be easy to eat only candy bars and burgers washed down with soda each day. It takes more planning and effort to eat nutritious meals.

So how do we plan and stick to a healthy diet? It is important to remember the main point of having a nutritious diet in the first place. Nutrition describes the process of giving the body the chemicals it needs. The chemicals useful to the body are called **nutrients**. Nutrients provide power and energy. The body needs nutrients in order to grow, repair itself, and recover from illness. Nutrition is a lifelong, around-the-clock process.

Breaking Down Nutrients

Nutrition cannot be separated from the digestive process—the process that breaks down food into nutrients and waste. The **digestive tract** is the system in the body that keeps this process going. It is an amazing system that usually hums along like a well-oiled machine. A nutritious diet keeps the process running smoothly. On the other hand, poor eating habits, illnesses, and diseases all cause digestive problems.

The entire digestive process for a forkful of food takes anywhere from 24 to 72 hours. Why such a long time? Because the digestive tract itself is long—longer than you are tall! In an average human adult, the digestive tract is about 30 feet (9 meters) long.

Let's take a brief trip through the digestive tract. Digestion begins in the mouth, when saliva, or spit, moistens your food and your teeth chew the food into small bits. When

Metric Conversion Chart

You can use the chart below to convert from U.S. measurements to the metric system.

Weight
1 ounce = 28 grams
1/2 pound = 8 ounces = 227 grams
1 pound = 0.45 kilogram
2.2 pounds = 1 kilogram

Liquid Volume
1 teaspoon = 5 milliliters
1 tablespoon = 15 milliliters
1 fluid ounce = 30 milliliters
1 cup = 240 milliliters
1 pint = 480 milliliters
1 quart = 0.95 liter

Length
1/4 inch = 0.6 centimeter
1/2 inch = 1.25 centimeters
1 inch = 2.5 centimeters

Temperature
100°F = 40°C
110°F = 45°C
350°F = 180°C
375°F = 190°C
400°F = 200°C
425°F = 220°C
450°F = 235°C

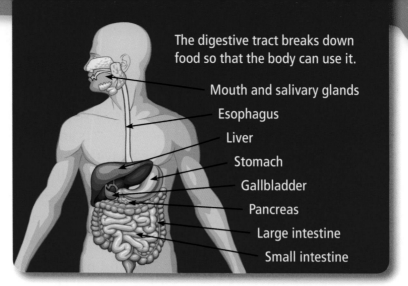

The digestive tract breaks down food so that the body can use it.

Mouth and salivary glands
Esophagus
Liver
Stomach
Gallbladder
Pancreas
Large intestine
Small intestine

you swallow, these bits pass into the **esophagus**, which is a muscular tube that pushes food down to the stomach. The stomach is a muscular pouch that contains chemicals to mix with and help digest the bits of food.

The gooey mixture of food and fluid from the stomach next passes into the **small intestine**. This is a long, wound-up tube that's about 20 feet (6 m) long. It's here that the mixture is broken into different nutrients. The nutrients are then absorbed into the bloodstream.

Digestion's final steps take place in the **large intestine**, where anything that the small intestine did not use becomes waste. The body absorbs most of the remaining water in the large intestine. The rest of the waste gets pushed out of the body. This completes the digestive process.

As your body digests food, it creates energy. People calculate the amount of energy created through digestion in

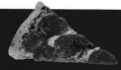

It takes between one and three days for a single slice of pizza to be completely digested.

In the mouth: 1 to 2 minutes

Down the esophagus: 4 to 6 minutes

Churned in the stomach: 1 to 6 hours

Moving through the small intestine: 2 to 9 hours

Moving through the large intestine: 1 to 3 days

terms of **calories**. Some people believe calories are the same as body fat. This is a mistake. A calorie is just a measurement of energy. Your body needs a certain amount of energy every day. It needs a certain number of calories in order to work properly. This is why cutting calories in order to lose weight can be unhealthy.

Getting the Important Nutrients

Your body produces some nutrients on its own. However, there are other nutrients that your body cannot make. How does it get these nutrients? This is where the food you eat becomes important. Nutrients that your body needs but cannot produce by itself are called *essential nutrients*.

There are six categories of essential nutrients. These are **carbohydrates**, **proteins**, **fats**, water, **vitamins**, and **minerals**. Different foods contain different essential nutrients. For this reason, a well-balanced diet includes sources of all the essential nutrients.

The idea of balancing a diet raises some questions. Which foods should we eat to meet our needs? How much of any one food should we eat? How do we know if our diet is healthy?

One way to answer these questions is to look at dietary guidelines, such as the Dietary Reference Intakes (DRI). There are five main sets of DRI guidelines. These are for males (by age group), females (by age group), infants, pregnant women, and breast-feeding women.

Why not have one set of guidelines for everyone? The answer is that dietary needs change for different people at different stages of life. The goal for everyone is good health and nutrition, but the requirements for good health and nutrition vary from person to person.

One tool for tracking nutrients is the Nutrition Facts label printed on a food's packaging. This label tells the amount of each nutrient in each serving of the food. It also tells what percentage of an average person's daily need that amount provides.

In addition to the Nutrition Facts label, another useful nutrition tool is called MyPyramid. MyPyramid ties together information about all of the different food groups. It helps people select nutritious food and balance wise food choices with reasonable serving sizes. It also promotes healthy physical activity. The U.S. government, the creator of MyPyramid, strongly recommends that everyone create an individualized pyramid. As noted earlier, age, sex, and level of physical activity strongly affect nutrition needs.

Let's take a look at the different nutrients that we all need to think about. First stop, carbohydrates.

MyPyramid is produced by the U.S. government. This user-friendly tool was created using information from many health and nutrition guidelines. You can find it online at www.mypyramid.gov.

Nutrition Facts

Serving Size 1 cup (228g)
Servings Per Container 2

Amount Per Serving

Calories 250	Calories from Fat 110
	% Daily Value*
Total Fat 12g	18%
Saturated Fat 3g	15%
Trans Fat 3g	
Cholesterol 30mg	10%
Sodium 470mg	20%
Potassium 700mg	20%
Total Carbohydrate 31g	10%
Dietary Fiber 0g	0%
Sugars 5g	
Protein 5g	

Vitamin A	4%
Vitamin C	2%
Calcium	20%
Iron	4%

* Percent Daily Values are based on a 2,000 calorie diet. Your Daily Values may be higher or lower depending on your calorie needs.

		Calories:	2,000	2,500
Total fat	Less than		65g	80g
Sat fat	Less than		20g	25g
Cholesterol	Less than		300mg	300mg
Sodium	Less than		2,400mg	2,400mg
Total Carbohydrate			300g	375g
Dietary Fiber			25g	30g

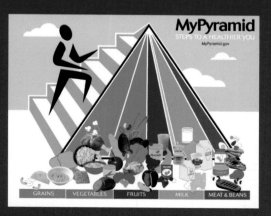

MyPyramid
STEPS TO A HEALTHIER YOU
MyPyramid.gov

GRAINS   VEGETABLES   FRUITS   MILK   MEAT & BEANS

Another tool you can use to be healthy is the Nutrition Facts label that is on most packaged foods sold in North America and England.

Myth: All carbohydrates make you fat.

Fact: Carbohydrates from fruit, vegetables, and whole-grain foods are the best diet aids—and they are your body's first resource for energy.

2 Carbs, Carbs, Marvelous Carbs

Carbohydrates ("carbs" for short) are the first nutrients digested by the body. This works out nicely, because carbs are the nutrients that power the digestive system. In fact, carbs power pretty much the entire body with the energy it needs. This includes the energy needed to keep your heart and lungs pumping. It also includes the energy it takes for you to move your muscles.

There are three main categories of carbohydrates. These are simple carbs, complex carbs, and dietary **fiber**. All three categories are necessary for the body.

Carbs That Are Simple and Sweet

The first carb category is *simple carbohydrates*. These are often called simple sugars. They are called "simple" because their **molecules** have simple structures. Simple sugars taste sweet, and your body can digest them quickly for fast energy.

The three most important simple sugars are **glucose**, **galactose**, and **fructose**. Glucose is your body's main energy source. It is found in all carbohydrates. The glucose in your bloodstream is often called **blood sugar**. The body uses some glucose for energy right away and stores some for later use. Extra glucose becomes body fat. Meanwhile, the body uses galactose to make brain cells. Galactose comes mainly from dairy products. Fructose, the third important simple sugar, is what makes fruits and some vegetables (such as sweet potatoes and onions) taste sweet. Like glucose, it is a useful energy source.

There is one other famous simple sugar: **sucrose**. This is the sugar that makes soda, candy, and many other foods tempting. It's true that sucrose, like all simple carbs, provides a quick boost of energy. However, many foods with sucrose have a low nutritional value. So, if you are looking for a snack that packs energy, you will do better eating a piece of fruit than a candy bar.

Carbs That Are Complex

After simple carbs, or simple sugars, the second carb category is *complex carbohydrates*. Complex carbohydrates are made of simple carbs linked together. Because there are more links in complex carbs than there are in simple carbs, it takes longer for your body to break them down. Also, because it takes longer to break them down, complex carbs enter the bloodstream at a slower, steadier pace. While they will not give you a burst of energy, they *will* supply steady energy over long periods of time.

Foods high in complex carbs taste more starchy than sweet. In fact, complex carbs are also called starches. There are two main types: natural starches and refined starches. You can find natural starches in foods such as whole-grain cereals, breads, and pastas. You can also find them in brown rice, oats, and nuts. You find refined starches in foods such as white rice and products made with processed flour.

Eating foods rich in natural starches instead of refined starches can help people lose weight. Eating natural starches makes us feel full more quickly, and for a longer period of time. Eating refined starches—such as the ones in chips and pizza—provides calories that don't fill us up for long. So we end up wanting to eat again sooner.

Complex carbs have a reputation for causing weight gain. This reputation is partly deserved. In most cases, however, people gain weight by eating too many high-carb meals (especially those high in refined starches) *as well as* failing to exercise. In general, it is best to eat whole grains and natural starches, and to combine this with other parts of a good diet and exercise program.

What Is a Whole Grain?

Bran: the outer skin of a grain kernel, loaded with fiber

Germ: the part of the kernel that grows into a plant and is filled with vitamins and minerals

Endosperm: the germ's food supply, made mostly of starch

For whole-grain foods, the entire kernel of grain is ground to make flour. It is the bran that makes this flour gritty, or slightly crunchy. Refined grains, like white rice and processed flour, are made of only the kernel's starchy endosperm. The bran and germ are tossed out. The refining process creates smoother flour, but it gets rid of nutritional value.

Bran

Endosperm

Germ

Fabulous Fiber

The third category of carbohydrates is fiber. Fiber is actually a type of complex carb. Unlike other carbs, your body cannot convert fiber into energy, so fiber has no calories. Fiber passes through the digestive tract and eventually comes out as waste. You might wonder, then, why is fiber valuable?

It turns out that fiber is an important part of any healthy diet. Fiber comes in two forms, *soluble fiber* and *insoluble fiber*. Soluble fiber dissolves in water during the digestive process, forming a gooey substance that slows down your body's use of glucose. Soluble fiber also sticks to some of the fat traveling in your small intestine and carries it through the rest of the digestive tract—eventually taking it out of the body as waste.

Insoluble fiber absorbs water like a sponge. This type of fiber helps control the movements of the small intestine. It also slows starch breakdown and the body's use of glucose. This gives your body plenty of time to extract the nutrients and send them where they need to go.

Insoluble fiber also helps bulk up and soften your waste, so that it passes more quickly through your large intestine. This decreases the time waste spends there (by the time food gets into your large intestine, it's nothing more than waste and bacteria that might be harmful to your body). Also, it's easier on your body to push out softer waste.

Most Americans do not eat enough fiber. A good amount of daily dietary fiber for boys between age 14 and 18 is

38 grams (about 1.4 oz), and for girls it is 26 grams (a little less than 1 oz). However, most Americans eat barely 11 grams (0.4 oz) of fiber a day.

Increasing your fiber often means little more than swapping one food product you already enjoy for a similar item with a higher fiber content. Be sure to raise your fiber content slowly. Because fiber speeds up the process that gets rid of waste, adding fiber too quickly can cause cramping and gas.

Fiber also helps lower the risk of certain diseases and promotes a healthier digestive process. It even helps you lose excess pounds! Fiber is good for you in more ways than you might have guessed at first.

Eating high-fiber cereal with lowfat or nonfat milk is a healthy way to add fiber to your diet.

3

Chew the Fat— But Just a Little Bit

Fat is the most misunderstood nutrient. Many people believe that the secret to a good diet is to stop eating fats completely. This idea comes from the misunderstanding that *fat-free* and *low-calorie* have the same meaning.

Remember, calories measure the *energy* in a certain food. Jelly beans and cookies are available in fat-free versions. However, they are still loaded with high-calorie processed sugar or refined flour (or both). Those are types of carbohydrates that can make you gain weight. It's not always a food's fat content that causes you to be unhealthy or pack on the pounds.

A second misunderstanding about fat is that fat in your diet is the same as body fat. This is not true. There are good and bad dietary fats, just as there are good and bad carbo-hydrates. The question is, how do you tell good and bad fats apart?

Good Fats, Bad Fats

The fats that we get from food are called **triglycerides**. These are the only fats that provide energy. They include both good and bad fats. Triglycerides can be sorted into three categories: **unsaturated fats**, **saturated fats**, and **trans fats**. What's important to know is that unsaturated fats are good, while saturated and trans fats are bad.

Moderate amounts of unsaturated fats have several ben-efits. They provide energy, help transport vitamins through your body, and help produce body fat that cushions organs. They are thought to lower **cholesterol** in the blood. (We'll learn about cholesterol later on.) Also, they have been shown to lower the risk of heart disease. Your body *needs* some unsaturated fats. This is why most physicians and dietitians recommend a *low-fat* rather than a *fat-free* diet.

Saturated fats and trans fats, on the other hand, are the reason fats have such a bad reputation. Both of these fats are linked to an increased risk for heart disease, stroke, and becoming dangerously overweight. They also raise the blood's cholesterol level. Saturated fats are in foods such as whole milk, butter, and some meats. Infants and very young children need a certain amount of saturated fat. After the age of two, though, people no longer need it.

Trans fats provide no benefits for anyone at any age. Unfortunately, we tend to eat a lot of these fats because they are what make cakes, cookies, and french fries taste so good.

Cholesterol and Other Fat-like Foods

There are other chemicals we eat that, though similar to fats, are also somewhat different. **Phospholipids** fall into this category. They provide no energy. Instead, they help your body work with fats. They allow triglycerides to mix with blood and digestion fluids. They also keep your blood smooth and reduce the risk of fat globs blocking blood flow and causing heart disease.

Sterols are other fat-like chemicals. Like phospholipids, sterols provide no energy but are still useful. Your body needs sterols for various reasons. The body makes most of the sterols it needs and only uses a little bit from food. The best-known sterol is cholesterol.

Cholesterol may be even more misunderstood than fat. What many people don't realize is that your body *makes* cholesterol. Your body also *needs* cholesterol. Cholesterol is used for many things, including producing healthy cell walls, helping with fat and vitamin digestion, and generating healthy fat that cushions internal organs.

It's easy to have too much cholesterol, however. When we eat too many foods that are high in cholesterol (such as meat, eggs, and high-fat dairy products), the body ends up with extra cholesterol. When this happens, the cholesterol clumps together and blocks blood flow. This can increase your risk of heart attack and stroke.

Remember this: with a healthy diet, your body produces the cholesterol it needs in just the right amount. It's a foolproof process until we humans overload the system.

4 Protein Power

Here are two cool protein facts: First, for most Americans, getting enough proteins is not a problem. Second, there are no "bad" proteins. We can get proteins from milk, cheese, eggs, yogurt, beef, chicken, fish, nuts, beans, and other foods. There are even proteins in fruits!

So, if protein is not a problem for most Americans, why is it important to know about it in order to have a nutritious diet? The body needs proteins just as it needs carbohydrates and fats. Proteins are necessary for growth, repair of cells, and various other purposes. Because of this, it is important to understand protein—and how we get proteins from food.

Important Functions of Proteins in the Body

1. *Structural proteins* affect what cells do and give different body parts their unique shapes.

2. *Regulatory proteins* help create new cells that replace old cells.

3. *Signal proteins* aid communication among nerve cells and between nerve and muscle cells.

4. *Defensive proteins* are part of your body's immune system.

5. Proteins are a key part of speeding up and slowing down chemical reactions.

6. If the body is desperate, proteins can be digested for energy—but this decreases muscles and is only done if there are not enough fats and carbohydrates.

Protein Essentials

Proteins are found in every human body part. Protein is an important part of every living cell. Water makes up most of the body, but if all the water in your body was removed, approximately 75 percent of your remaining weight would be protein.

So where do these proteins come from? The stomach first breaks down protein-rich food into molecules during digestion. These molecules are still too big to use, so they are digested further in the small intestine, into small molecules called **amino acids**. All in all, there are 22 different amino acids that your body needs.

Of these 22 amino acids, nine must come from food because your body cannot manufacture them on its own. These nine are called *essential amino acids*. Also, your body cannot store proteins as it does extra fats and carbohydrates. So it's important—*essential*, you might say—to eat proteins every day.

Animal and Plant Proteins

Proteins that come from animal sources are sometimes called *complete proteins*. These proteins contain all nine essential amino acids. Proteins from vegetables are sometimes called **incomplete proteins** because they lack one or more of the nine essential amino acids. This can be a problem for vegetarians, but is easily corrected by eating a variety of plants and grains with different proteins. After all, you don't need to eat all nine essential amino acids at one sitting! Once again, as with other nutrients, the key with proteins is *balance*—a balanced diet with a variety of protein sources.

Soybeans are the exception when it comes to plant proteins being short on amino acids. Soybeans provide all nine essential amino acids. What's more, soybeans have no cholesterol and are high in dietary fiber. For vegetarians, soybeans and food products made with soybeans (such as the tofu and other items in the picture) are must-have daily menu items.

5 Don't Forget Water, Vitamins, and Minerals

Water might seem like a strange nutrient because it provides no energy. But water is essential to good health. Water is the basis for every bodily fluid, and it is involved in every process connected to nutrition. Your body would be unable to get energy from carbs and fats without water.

Water accounts for at least 60 percent of total body weight. So, for example, if someone weighs 180 pounds (82 kg), at least 108 pounds (49 kg) of that weight is probably water. It's important for good health to maintain that percentage. In other words, keep drinking water!

Dehydration is no joke. Even mild dehydration—a loss of 1 to 2 percent of the body's necessary water—can cause problems such as headaches, fatigue, and loss of concentration. A 10 percent drop in your body's water weight can be life-threatening, and a 20 percent drop can lead to death.

Drink Your Water!

How much water should you drink every day? It depends on your body, diet, exercise level, and climate. It is a good idea to drink a tall glass of water before going on a bike ride, playing soccer with friends, or even taking an important test.

Some foods help you get the water you need. These foods are called "water-rich" foods. Apples, broccoli, cucumbers, and oranges are examples of water-rich foods.

When you drink to resupply your body's water, it is important to remember that not all drinks are equally nutritious. Soda, for example, fills you with fluids but also has sugar, which adds pounds along with water. Sports drinks and vitamin waters also often have more sugar than soda has. Energy drinks are even worse. On top of a heavy dose of sugar, they include caffeine. Although doctors think that reasonable amounts of caffeine are harmless, caffeine may increase urine output for those who do not usually have it in their diet. This *could* lead to a loss of fluid, and increase the risk of dehydration.

Here's an equation that helps you find out how much water your body needs. If you're moderately active, multiply your body weight in pounds by 0.5. (If you're very active, multiply by 0.6.) The figure you come up with is your daily water requirement in ounces. For example, if you are moderately active and weigh 115 pounds (52 kg), you should drink 57.5 ounces (1.6 kg) of water, or around seven eight-ounce glasses (1.7 liters, total) each day.

Vitamins and Minerals Pack a Punch

Although you need a large daily volume of nutrients such as water, there are other nutrients that the body only requires in small amounts. Vitamins and minerals fall into this category. You shouldn't make the mistake of thinking that vitamins and minerals are unimportant. A diet lacking essential vitamins and minerals can cause serious problems.

Vitamins come from living things, such as fruits, vegetables, or animals. There are 11 specific vitamins that your body must have in order to live. These are called essential vitamins.

Some vitamins dissolve in water. When there are too many of these vitamins in your body, the extras are mixed with water and pass out of the body in urine. Other vitamins dissolve in fat. Excess vitamins of this kind are stored in body fat.

Unlike vitamins, minerals come from *nonliving* sources such as soil, rocks, or water. Like vitamins, minerals are divided into two groups. There are seven minerals that your body needs more than 100 milligrams of each day. There are nine minerals that your body needs less than 20 milligrams of each day. Even though your body needs only small amounts of minerals, they have key roles in helping the body function well.

Antioxidants are special vitamins and minerals. Scientists believe that antioxidants protect body cells from dangerous chemicals that speed up the aging process and cause heart disease and cancer. At this time, scientists are not exactly sure how or why antioxidants work.

Important Vitamins and Minerals

The following table has examples of just a few important vitamins and minerals, along with the roles they play in the body.

Vitamins	Roles and Purposes
Vitamin A	Helps keep both vision and skin healthy
Vitamin B family (B1, B2, and so forth)	Helps convert carbohydrates into glucose and break down fats and proteins
Vitamin C	Strengthens the body's immune system and healing processes
Vitamin D	Allows the body to absorb and process the mineral calcium
Vitamin E	Contributes to a healthy reproductive system and helps build strong nerves and muscles
Vitamin K	Produces proteins that allow your blood to clot when you get cut
Minerals	**Roles and Purposes**
Calcium	Supplies material to build bones and teeth; also helps the heart, nerves, muscles, and other body parts function
Iron	Among other things, helps blood cells carry oxygen to body parts and carry carbon dioxide away
Magnesium	Helps build bones and teeth, create energy in digestion, and promote healthy functioning of organs
Potassium	Needed for growth, building muscle, helping the nervous system, keeping blood pressure stable, and allowing kidneys to function

Myth: The best way to lose weight is to stop eating.

Fact: Starvation is a serious eating disorder that can kill you. To lose weight and keep it off, eat a healthy diet and exercise for 60 minutes a day.

6 Exercise Your Options

Give your body the right foods in the right amounts, and it knows exactly what to do with them. It digests the foods and uses them for energy, growth, fighting illness, and other things. Give yourself too much food, however, and you end up with too much fuel—and too many calories. Your body takes the extra fuel and converts it into body fat.

Your body really doesn't like having a lot of fat, though. A little bit, as we have already mentioned, has its uses. Body fat provides padding for your internal organs and allows your body to store energy. If too much fat builds up, however, it can bring about a number of dangers such as diabetes, heart disease, high blood pressure, high cholesterol, strokes, or certain cancers.

Tackling Extra Weight

What can you do about excess weight? It's actually pretty simple. You can eat fewer unnecessary calories and exercise more. If you increase exercise beyond your normal routine, while at the same time eating less, your body will dip into stored energy that has become fat. Once you return to a stable weight that's right for you, your body will return to normal.

Exercising raises some of the same questions as dieting. How much is enough? What is a healthy level of exercise? Can you do too much of it? While it is possible to exercise too much, most people have the problem of not exercising enough. The U.S. Department of Health and Human Services recommends at least 60 minutes of exercise each day for children and teens in order to promote good health and reduce the risk of life-threatening diseases. Teens may also add muscle-strengthening activities (children do not need this). Exercising slightly more than 60 minutes a day can also help teens and adults lose weight.

All this exercising might seem like a lot. Don't worry— you don't need to do it all at once. If you are aiming to do 60 minutes a day, you can break up the time into 10-minute bits. Take your dog for a 10-minute walk, ride your bike for 10 minutes to the corner store, and help out at home by vacuuming for 10 minutes. That makes 30 minutes of exercise right there. You'd be halfway to your 60-minute goal before even jogging or playing sports. That doesn't sound so bad, does it?

Exercise: Revving the Engines

Exercising has health benefits beyond just keeping your weight steady. Regular physical activity that increases the heart rate actually revs up every process in the body, including blood circulation. This also means a more consistent supply of energy to the brain.

Exercise also reduces stress by releasing chemicals in your body to make you feel good. When you exercise heavily, your body responds to the extra effort the same way it responds to pain: it releases chemicals that can help ease your pain and even give you a sense of well-being.

Strange as it might sound, burning energy through exercise gives you *more* energy. Exercise makes your body burn energy more steadily. It steadies blood flow, too. This jumpstarts a range of healthy developments—such as lower heart rate, blood pressure, and cholesterol levels. Stable blood flow also gets essential nutrients to their destinations more reliably, which helps boost your immune system. When your body is better equipped to fight off illness, you spend more time feeling healthy and happy.

The reason to eat a nutritionally balanced diet and get plenty of exercise is so that you can live a long and healthy life. It's certainly a reachable goal—as long as you don't mess up your chances. What do we mean by this? Eating too much junk food is one thing that gets in the way of a long, healthy life. Failing to get enough exercise is another. Trying to lose weight with a popular but nonscientific diet or by lowering your calorie intake to unhealthy levels are potentially dangerous solutions that can get in the way of true healthiness and happiness.

Remember, the purpose of a nutritious diet is to give your body the nutrients and energy it needs so you can enjoy life. When it comes to nutrition, be creative, be clever, and be careful—but always enjoy the foods that fuel your body and your life.

Balance and moderation are the two keys to eating nutritiously and having a healthy body.

Glossary

amino acids: The building blocks of protein molecules. Humans require 22 different amino acids, nine of which must come from food. These nine amino acids are called *essential amino acids*.

antioxidants: Special vitamins and minerals that protect against damage and destruction of cells in the body.

blood sugar: Glucose (a form of sugar) in the bloodstream.

calories: Measurement units for the energy available from food.

carbohydrates: Sugars, starches, and most fibers; one of the six classes of nutrients. *Simple carbohydrates* are naturally occurring sugars, such as those found in fruit; they are a source of quick energy. *Complex carbohydrates*, which provide longer-lasting energy, are found in most grain products and many vegetables, including potatoes.

cholesterol: A fat-like substance that is an essential element in body-tissue cell membranes. Blood transports cholesterol through the body. Excessively high cholesterol levels are known to increase the risk of heart disease.

dehydration: The condition that results when the body does not have enough water for its normal functions. Extreme dehydration can be life-threatening.

digestive tract: The system in the body that food flows through during digestion.

esophagus: A tube of muscle that moves food from the throat to the stomach. The esophagus is part of the digestive tract.

fats: One of the six essential nutrient groups. This group includes *unsaturated fats* (fats found mainly in vegetable oils that have benefits to the body), *saturated fats* (animal fats that can increase the risk of heart disease if eaten in quantities above recommendations), and *trans fats* (unsaturated fatty acids that have been linked to heart disease and should be avoided).

fiber: A special carbohydrate that travels through the digestive tract to help waste pass out of the body more easily. *Soluble fiber* dissolves in water; *insoluble fiber* does not. Both types are important to digestion.

fructose, galactose, and **glucose:** Simple carbohydrates (simple sugars) found in foods. Fructose is found in fruits and vegetables. Galactose is found mostly in dairy products. Glucose is the sugar that other carbohydrates are broken down into for quick energy.

large intestine: The last part of the digestive tract where wastes are created.

minerals: One of the six classes of nutrients. The body needs only small amounts of minerals.

molecules: The smallest divisions of substances that are still considered to be those substances.

nutrients: Substances needed by the body for energy and tissue building. The six classes of nutrients are carbohydrates, protein, fats, vitamins, minerals, and water. *Essential nutrients* are those that the body needs to get by eating and drinking.

phospholipids: Fat-like substances that are part of a balanced diet and aid in fat digestion.

proteins: Chains of amino acids; one of the six classes of nutrients. Found in animal products, such as eggs and meat, and in certain vegetables, grains, and beans. Animal proteins are often called *complete proteins* because they contain all nine essential amino acids. Most plant proteins are *incomplete proteins* because they do not have all nine.

small intestine: The long wound-up tube that food passes into from the stomach; the part of the digestive tract where nutrients are absorbed into the bloodstream.

sterols: Fat-like substances found in the tissues of many plants and animal foods; the best-known sterol is cholesterol.

sucrose: A sweet-tasting simple carbohydrate (simple sugar) with low nutritional value.

triglycerides: Fats in the diet that provide energy.

vitamins: Substances found in tiny amounts in plant and animal foods; one of the six classes of nutrients.

Find Out More

Books

Claybourne, Anna. *Healthy Eating: Diet and Nutrition.* Portsmouth, NH: Heinemann, 2008.

Douglas, Ann, and Julie Douglas. *Body Talk: The Straight Facts on Fitness, Nutrition, and Feeling Great about Yourself!* 2nd edition. Toronto: Maple Tree Press, 2006.

Favor, Lesli J. *Food as Foe: Nutrition and Eating Disorders.* New York: Marshall Cavendish, 2008.

Favor, Lesli J. *Weighing In: Nutrition and Weight Management.* New York: Marshall Cavendish, 2008.

Rinzler, Carol Ann. *Nutrition for Dummies.* 4th edition. Hoboken, NJ: Wiley Publishing, 2006.

Schlosser, Eric, and Charles Wilson. *Chew On This: Everything You Don't Want to Know about Fast Food.* Boston: Houghton Mifflin, 2006.

Shryer, Donna. *Body Fuel: A Guide to Good Nutrition.* New York: Marshall Cavendish, 2008.

Shryer, Donna. *Peak Performance: Sports Nutrition.* New York: Marshall Cavendish, 2008.

Websites

The American Dietetic Association
(Food and Nutrition Website)
http://www.eatright.org

KidsHealth (The Nemours Foundation)
http://kidshealth.org

MyPyramid
http://www.mypyramid.gov

Index

Page numbers for photographs and illustrations are in **boldface**.